Walt Disney's Pinocchio

A Disney Read-Aloud Film Classic

Harmony Books/New York

Published by Harmony Books, a division of Crown Publishers, Inc., One Park Avenue, New York, New York 10016, and simultaneously in Canada by General Publishing Company Limited

HARMONY BOOKS and colophon are trademarks of Crown Publishers, Inc.

Manufactured in the United States of America

Grateful acknowledgment is hereby made to Bourne Co. for permission to reprint lyrics from *When You Wish Upon a Star, Little Wooden Head,* and *Give a Little Whistle.* Music by Leigh Harline, words by Ned Washington, copyright 1940 by Bourne Co., copyright renewed.

Library of Congress Cataloging in Publication Data
Main entry under title:

Walt Disney's Pinocchio.

(Disney read-aloud film clssic)
Based on the original story by Carlo Lorenzini.
Summary: Text and color stills from the film present the adventures of the puppet boy whose nose grew whenever he told a lie.
[1. Fairy tales. 2. Puppets—Fiction] I. Lorenzini,
Carlo, 1826–1890. Avventure de Pinocchio. II. Walt
Disney Productions. III. Title: Pinocchio. IV. Series.
PZ8.P59   1982   [Fic]   82-3057
ISBN: 0-517-544601   AACR2
       0-517-54461X (paperback)

10 9 8 7 6 5 4 3 2 1
First Edition

Introduction

Pinocchio, which was made in 1940, was Walt Disney's most ambitious project. Even after the innovative techniques developed for *Snow White, Pinocchio* demanded a whole new approach. Different ways of handling paints and pastels and complicated airbrush and drybrush methods were explored to capture the extraordinarily detailed and colorful effects.

Disney attempted many spectacular shots using the multiplane camera. Woolie Reitherman, who worked on Disney's first full-length animated feature, had no doubts about their achievement: "There's a very impressive tracking shot at the start of *Pinocchio,* in which the camera pans across the sleeping village and ducks between buildings and down to the street to focus on Jiminy Cricket. The cameramen were so creative with the use of angles as well as the use of a dozen planes for a three-dimensional effect that they ran up a bill of twenty-five thousand dollars for a half-minute shot. And that was just for the photography."

Fresh from the success of *Snow White,* Disney went ahead with this unprecedented new project, but after six months he was obliged to interrupt production. There were basic problems with the character and depiction of Pinocchio. Illustrations from Carlo Collodi's 1881 classic children's story showed him as a puppet. But Disney knew it was vital for audience involvement to make Pinocchio more boylike and, at the same time, to retain his essential jerky woodenness. To heighten the contrast, the other characters were made more flamboyant. In fact, W. C. Fields, a notoriously acid critic, complained that the explosively villainous puppet-master, Stromboli, actually moved too much!

Jiminy Cricket also had to undergo a radical transformation from the original, where he plays a minor but critical role before being crushed underfoot. Awarding him an 18-karat gold badge that reads "Official Conscience" immediately enlarged Jiminy's part, but his physical size still presented quite a challenge to the art department. They had to make him both likeable and large enough to be noticed on screen with the other characters, who were often larger than life. Clever use of camera angle resolved the practical problem of stature, and two hit songs, "When You Wish Upon a Star" and "Give a Little Whistle," assured Jiminy of star status.

Despite the variety and vitality of the cast, the bubbling humor, the outstanding special effects, and the radiant depth of the color, the film was not a box-office success when it was released in February 1940. Despite the acclaim of the critics, the public may have found it hard to respond to a cartoon fable with World War II on the horizon. But rereleases have confirmed the quality of the film and have attracted millions of people. *Pinocchio* remains one of Walt Disney's enduring masterpieces.

P. Sidey

One night a long time ago, Jiminy Cricket's
travels took him to a quaint little village.

The only sign of life was the lighted window in
the shop of Geppetto, the wood-carver.

"Well, you've never seen such a place," says Jiminy. "It was full of the most fantastic clocks, music boxes, and toys—all carved out of wood and each one a work of art."

"There was shelf after shelf of toys, and then something else caught my eye. It was one of those marionettes, all strings and joints."

"As I sat on the marionette's nose, I heard
someone coming down the stairs," says Jiminy.

"It won't take much longer," says Geppetto.
"A little more paint and he's all finished."

Geppetto adds a smiling mouth and says, "Now
I have just the name for you: Pinocchio."

Geppetto and his cat Figaro spend hours playing with the marionette.

"Come now," says Geppetto, "we'll try you out."

He begins singing:
"Little wooden head, go play your part,
Bring a little joy to every heart.
Little do you know—and yet it's true—
That I am very proud of you."

Later, as Geppetto and Figaro are about to go to bed, they see a bright star.

"Look, Figaro, a wishing star," says Geppetto, and he makes a wish:

*"I wish I may, I wish I might,
Have the wish I wish tonight.*

I wish that my little Pinocchio might be a *real* boy!"

Meanwhile, downstairs, the Blue Fairy appears.

Waving her wand, the Fairy says, "Little puppet made of pine, wake! The gift of life is thine!"

"I can move! I can walk! I can talk!" exclaims
Pinocchio.

"I have given you life," says the Fairy, "because tonight Geppetto wished for a real boy. But to make his wish come true you must prove yourself brave, honest, and unselfish."

"Jiminy," she says, "you will be his conscience and help him choose between right and wrong. A conscience is the still, small voice that people don't always listen to. For this you will become Sir Jiminy. Pinocchio, always let your conscience be your guide."

With a wave, the Fairy was gone.

Jumping onto Geppetto's violin, Jiminy sings:
  "When you get into trouble
  And don't know what to do
  Give a little whistle,
  Give a little whistle.
  Take the straight and
Narrow path, and if
You start to slide
Give a little whistle
And always let your
Conscience be your guide."

Awakened by the singing, Geppetto and Figaro
tiptoe downstairs.

"Here I am," shouts Pinocchio. "The Blue Fairy came and I'm going to be a real boy."

"A real boy," says Geppetto. "It's my wish come true."

Jiminy and the music-box dancers celebrate.

Geppetto, Pinocchio, and Figaro cuddle up in bed.

"Now, son," says Geppetto, "close your eyes and go to sleep. Tomorrow, you've got to go to school to learn things and become clever."

The next morning Geppetto dresses Pinocchio
and sends him off to school with an apple for
the teacher.

The sly fox, Honest John, and his friend, Gideon, stroll down the street.

"Listen to the merry laughter of little innocent children wending their way to school," snarls Honest John.

"Well, well, well," says Honest John, seeing the poster for the marionette show. "So Stromboli is back in town. Remember, Giddy, the time I tied strings on you and passed you off as a puppet?" he asks.

"Look, Giddy," shouts Honest John. "It's a
wooden boy. A live puppet without strings."

The wily fox has an idea.

"A thing like that ought to be worth a fortune,"
he says. "If we play our cards right, we'll be
millionaires or my name isn't Honest John."

Honest John stops Pinocchio and tries to trick
him into joining the marionette show.

"I'm speaking, my boy, of bright lights, music, applause . . . fame!" says the fox.

"But I'm going . . ." Pinocchio protests.

"Straight to the top, my boy," says Honest John.

Jiminy tries to stop Pinocchio.

"Do you remember what the Blue Fairy said about your conscience? Well, follow it now and don't go."

But the excitement of the theater is too much for
Pinocchio and he joins the troupe.

Night falls and still Pinocchio has not returned
from school.

"Oh, where could he be at this time of night?"
cries Geppetto.

After the show, Stromboli pays Pinocchio with a
gold coin.

"Thank you!" says Pinocchio. "I'll run right
home and tell my father."

"Home? This cage will be your home," roars
Stromboli. "You work for me now!"

"No, no, no!" cries Pinocchio, as Stromboli
locks him in the cage.

Pinocchio calls for Jiminy.

"Oh, Jiminy, where are you?"

Jiminy appears and says, "Don't worry, Pinocchio, we'll have you out of here in no time."

But the lock is rusty and Jiminy knows only a miracle will release Pinocchio.

Suddenly the Blue Fairy appears in a brilliant star.

"Pinocchio," she asks, "why didn't you go to school?"

Pinocchio lies, "Well, I met two monsters with green eyes and they tied me up . . . and they wanted to chop me into firewood."

Pinocchio's nose starts growing.

"My nose!" he cries.

The Blue Fairy tells him, "Perhaps you haven't been telling the truth. A little lie keeps on growing and growing."

"I'll never lie again," promises Pinocchio.

"This is the last time I can help you," the Blue
Fairy says as she opens the lock.

Jiminy and Pinocchio escape and run toward town.

Back in town, Honest John, Gideon, and a shady coachman are passing the evening at the Red Lobster Inn.

"How would you like to make some *real* money?" asks the coachman. "I'm looking for little boys to take to Pleasure Island."

The coachman assures the fox that he runs no
risk because the boys can never return from
Pleasure Island—as *boys*. Honest John and
Gideon go out to look for a victim, and who
should they find but Pinocchio!

Honest John tricks Pinocchio onto the coach.
Jiminy secretly jumps on board too.

Pinocchio meets Lampwick, who asks, "Have you ever been to Pleasure Island? They say it's wonderful there. You can eat and drink and tear the whole place apart if you want."

"It sounds like fun," says Pinocchio.

The coach lets the boys off at a boat ready to
set off for the mysterious Pleasure Island.

When the boat lands, the children run toward
the fabulous amusements to play and demolish
the carnival area.

The Pleasure Island carnival ground in ruins,
Pinocchio and Lampwick explore the other
pleasures of the island.

Jiminy, who has fallen behind the boys, grows suspicious. Something is not right here, he thinks.

Jiminy is very alarmed and whistles vainly for Pinocchio.

"I've got to find him," he says.

Meanwhile, Pinocchio and Lampwick live it up.

"Where do you think all the other boys are, Lampwick?" asks Pinocchio.

"Don't worry about it. They're around. This is
the life, isn't it?" asks Lampwick.

"So this is where I find you. Smoking. Playing pool. You're coming home with me!" says an angry Jiminy.

"But, Jiminy, Lampwick is my best friend," pleads Pinocchio.

"Your best friend! Well, I'm your conscience. I'm leaving; you can come if you want," says Jiminy.

"Aw, let that dumb beetle go," says Lampwick.
"Have another beer."

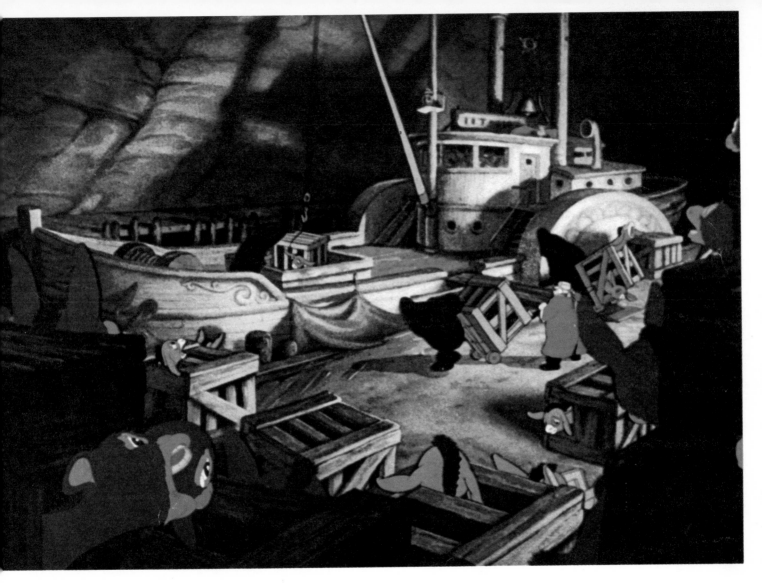

Jiminy decides to take the next boat home and
sees the coachman loading crates of donkeys
onto the boat.

Where on earth did all those donkeys come
from? he wonders.

Jiminy hears the coachman talking to one of the donkeys.

"Please, sir," says the donkey, "I don't want to be a donkey. I want to go home to my mother."

"You boys had your fun and now you have to pay," answers the coachman.

The boys are being turned into donkeys! Jiminy races to find Pinocchio.

"That little beetle thought something bad was
going to happen to us. What does he think I am,
a jackass?" asks Lampwick.

"He was right. Just feel your ears." Pinocchio
laughs.

Lampwick sees what has happened to him.

"Help, help!" he cries. "Call that beetle—call anybody!"

Jiminy returns just in time.

"Oh, Jiminy, I was wrong. Please help me!" says Pinocchio.

Together they escape and swim back to the mainland.

But when they get to town, Geppetto's house is
dark and full of cobwebs.

Pinocchio and Jiminy sit on the steps. Pinocchio
is very worried.

"Father's gone. Maybe something awful has
happened to him."

Suddenly a bird drops a message on the steps.

"It says your father went looking for you and was swallowed by a whale called Monstro,"

Jiminy reads aloud. "But he's still alive, inside the whale at the bottom of the sea."

Pinocchio, determined to find his father, runs toward the cliffs.

Jiminy tries to stop him and says, "Monstro is so big, he swallows ships in one gulp."

But they both know they must find Geppetto and they jump into the sea.

"Goodness, what a big place," says Pinocchio,
as they walk on the ocean bottom.

Pinocchio calls out, "Father, Father!"

"Mr. Geppetto, Mr. Geppetto. Oh, pardon me,
ladies," says Jiminy to two fish.

"Good day! Are you acquainted with Monstro
the whale?" Jiminy asks a clam.

Pinocchio and Jiminy wander over the ocean
floor, talking to all the fish, but no one knows
where to find Monstro the whale.

As Monstro sleeps, a little boat bobs about in his
stomach.

Inside the boat, Geppetto says to Figaro, "We can't hold out much longer. I never thought I'd starve to death in a whale's belly. There isn't a fish left."

Monstro wakes up hungry and chases a school
of fish, which surge into his mouth with a rush
and a roar.

Pinocchio and Jiminy watch with horror as the
huge black shape of Monstro bears down on
them. They are thrown apart and Pinocchio is
sucked over Monstro's teeth and into the whale.

Pinocchio clings onto the fish as they are swept
down into the great whale's belly.

"Help me, Figaro, here's a heavy fish," says
Geppetto.

"Hello, Father," calls Pinocchio.

"Pinocchio! It's you!" shouts Geppetto.

"My son. I'm so happy to see you."

"Me too, Father," says Pinocchio.

"You're soaking wet," says Geppetto. "You mustn't catch cold. Why are you here?"

"I came to save you," answers Pinocchio.

"Pinocchio! Those ears! What's happened to you?" asks the startled Geppetto.

"That's nothing. I've got a tail, too," says Pinocchio.

"Well, never mind now," says Geppetto. "Old Geppetto has his little boy and nothing else matters . . . except escaping. I've built a raft, but I've tried every way to get out and nothing has worked."

"All we can do is cook the fish on the fire I've made," says Geppetto.

But Pinocchio has an idea.

"A fire—that's it," he says. "We'll make a lot of smoke and make Monstro sneeze. Then he'll have to open his mouth."

Pinocchio's plan works. Monstro sneezes, his mouth opens, and they paddle the raft as quickly as they can toward the opening.

"Faster, faster," says Pinocchio.

"It won't work," cries Geppetto. "We'll never get past those teeth."

"Hang on!" shouts Pinocchio.

The raft shoots out of the whale's mouth and
bobs around on the ocean's surface.

The angry Monstro dives to the bottom.

"He's after us!" cry Geppetto and Pinocchio.

Monstro surfaces under the raft, throwing
everybody into the sea.

"Father, Father!" cries Pinocchio.

"Swim for shore, Pinocchio. Save yourself," says Geppetto.

But Pinocchio must save his father and swims with the exhausted Geppetto toward the shore.

The great effort has proved too much for poor
Pinocchio, and Geppetto finds him lying face
down in a pool on the beach.

Geppetto carries his son back home.

"Oh, my boy. My brave little boy," he sobs.

As the candle burns by the dead Pinocchio,
Jiminy wipes his eyes.

Suddenly a bright blue light shines on Pinocchio.

The Blue Fairy's voice comes out of the light:

"Prove yourself brave, honest, and unselfish and
some day you will be a real boy! Awake,
Pinocchio, awake!"

The light disappears and Pinocchio moves. He
has been transformed into a *real* boy.

"You're alive—and you *are* a real boy," says
Jiminy.

"A real live boy. This calls for a celebration,"
Geppetto says.

The happy Figaro shares a kiss with Cleo, the
goldfish.

All the clocks and music boxes start chiming and
playing while Geppetto and Pinocchio dance.

9217

Jiminy watches this happy scene and looks up toward the brightest star in the sky.

"When you wish upon a star,
Makes no difference who you are,

Anything your heart desires
Will come to you.

"Thank you, Blue Fairy," he says. "Pinocchio really deserves to become a real boy."